EL RATONCITO PEQUEÑO

THE LITTLE MOUSE

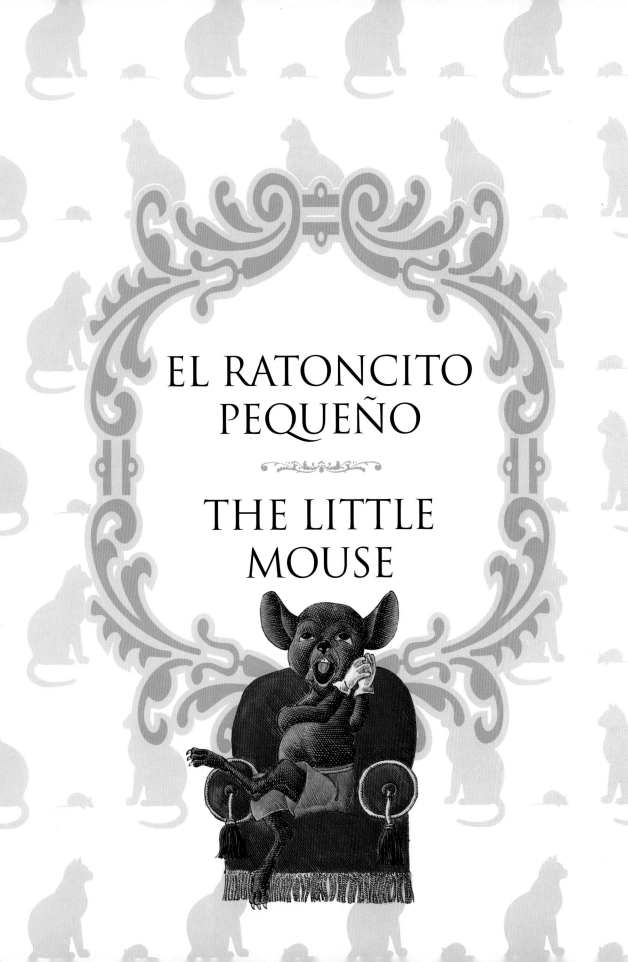

UN RATONCITO PEQUEÑO

A NICE LITTLE MOUSE

SIN MALICIA
TODAVÍA,

WITH AN
INNOCENT WAY,

AL DESPERTAR DE SU SUEÑO

WOKE UP FROM HIS DREAM

SE SENTÓ EN SU
CUARTO UN DÍA.

AND SAT DOWN
ONE DAY.

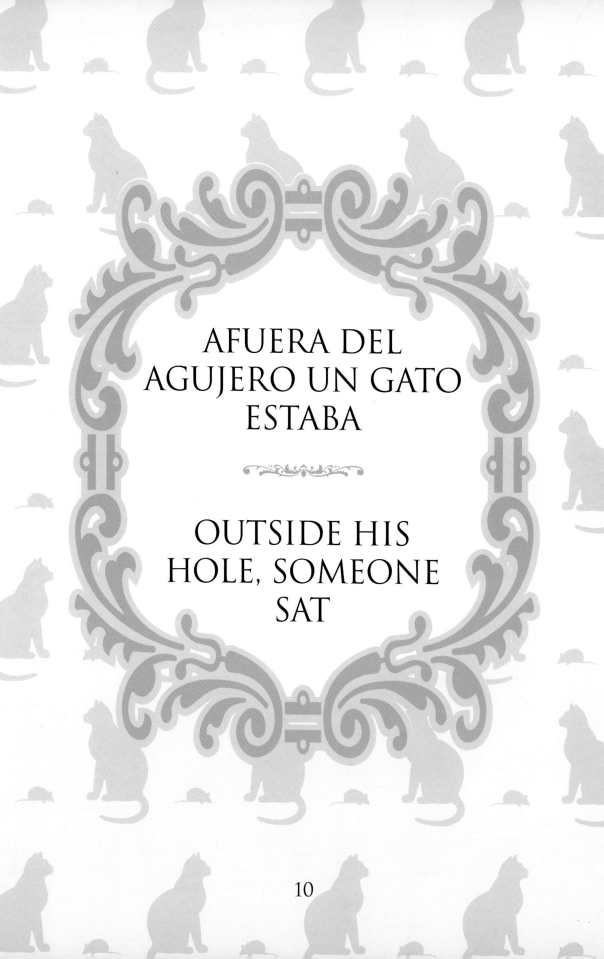

AFUERA DEL
AGUJERO UN GATO
ESTABA

OUTSIDE HIS
HOLE, SOMEONE
SAT

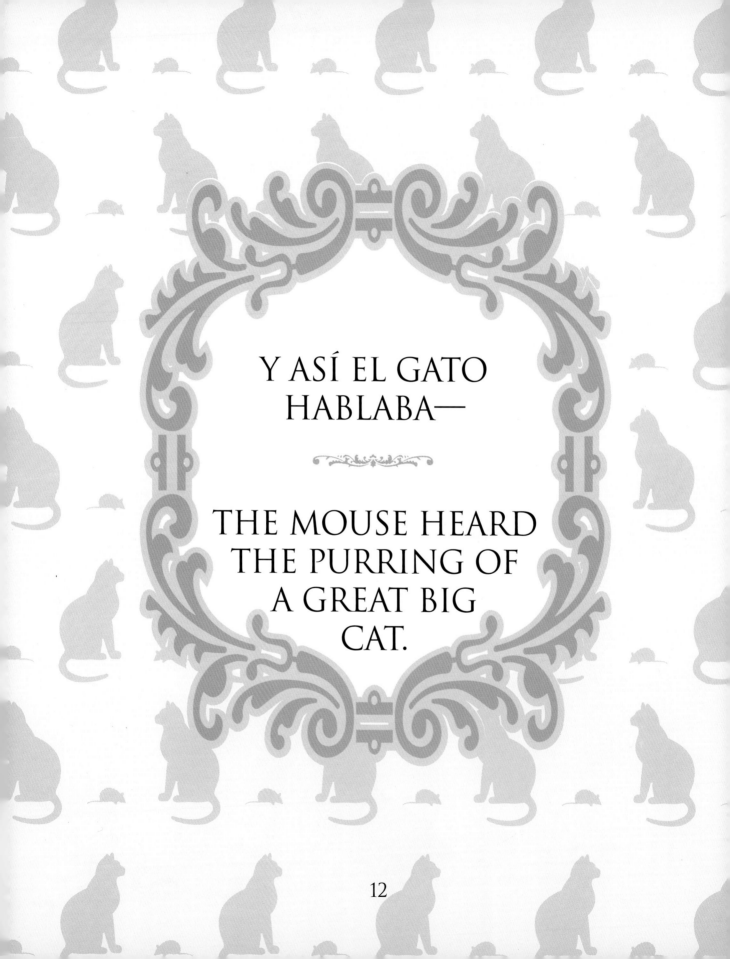

Y ASÍ EL GATO
HABLABA—

THE MOUSE HEARD
THE PURRING OF
A GREAT BIG
CAT.

SAL,
RATONCITO,

COME OUT, LITTLE
MOUSEY,

QUE TE QUIERO
ACARICIAR.

I WANT YOU TO
BE MY PET.

Y ESTE DULCE
EXQUISITO

I HAVE THIS FANCY
CANDY

18

TE LO QUIERO
REGALAR.

WHICH YOU WILL
LIKE, I BET.

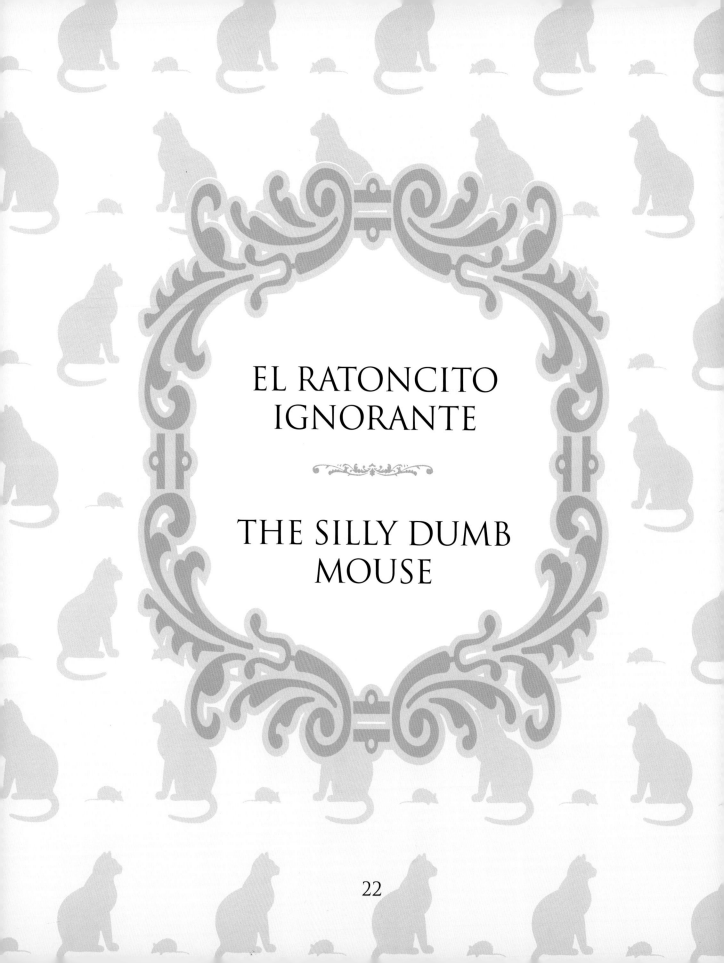

EL RATONCITO
IGNORANTE

THE SILLY DUMB
MOUSE

DE SU AGUJERO
SALIÓ

LEFT HIS HOLE FOR
A MUNCH

Y EL GATO EN EL
INSTANTE

AND
THE CAT IN AN
INSTANT

¡SE LO COMIÓ!

ATE HIM FOR
LUNCH.

POBRECITO
RATONCITO.

POOR LITTLE
MOUSE.

NOTE TO READERS

When I was very young, my mother taught me to recite poems, sing songs, and read stories in both English and Spanish. I have never forgotten these wonderful experiences with language.

One of my favorite poems was *El Ratoncito Pequeño*. When I went to my friend José Cisneros and asked him to do the drawings, I was elated to learn that he also had learned *El Ratoncito* as a child and could still recite it from memory. Many of my friends know the poem as well, but no one yet has been able to tell me where it originated. Perhaps you know?

Encourage your child to memorize *El Ratoncito Pequeño / The Little Mouse* in Spanish and in English. You will be surprised at how quickly your child can learn this poem. Maybe—like it was for me—the poem will be a part of their memories for the rest of their lives!

—*Pipina Salas-Porras*

NOTE ABOUT THE TRANSLATION

Nursery rhymes are for children. Thus, our goal in translating *El Ratoncito Pequeño* was to bring to the English the same playfulness with language and rhyme that the Spanish enjoys. A literal translation, of course, would not work.

We consulted with a number of writers and Spanish-speakers, and we kid-tested all of our variations. We were never 100% satisfied, but we think our current translation is the best of the bunch. If our readers disagree, send along your suggestions and we will consider them for the second printing.

—*The Publishers*

For more information, contact Cinco Puntos Press at 1 800 566-9072 or visit our website at www.cincopuntos.com

Cover design, book design, and typesetting by Geronimooo Design of El Paso, Texas.
Thanks to Joe Hayes and Jenna Camp for help with the translation and to Suzy Morris for her masterful hand in production.

EL RATONCITO PEQUEÑO / THE LITTLE MOUSE

FIRST EDITION

10 9 8 7 6 5 4 3 2 1

Library of Congress Cataloging-in-Publication Data

Salas-Porras, Pipina, 1926-
  [Ratoncito pequeno. English & Spanish]
  El ratoncito pequeno = The little mouse : a nursery rhyme in Spanish and English / as remembered by Pipina Salas-Porras ; illustrated by Jose Cisneros.—1st ed.
    p. cm.
  ISBN 0-938317-56-3
  1. Nursery rhymes. 2. Children's poetry. [1. Nursery rhymes.
  2. Spanish language materials—Bilingual.] I. Title: Little mouse. II.
Cisneros, Jose, 1910-   . ill. III. Title.
  PZ74.3 .S29 2001
  861'.7—dc21
                        00-047569